Adapted by Louise Gikow

Based on the motion picture screenplay
by Jeffrey Price & Peter S. Seaman

Based on the book by Dr. Seuss

RANDOM HOUSE NEW YORK

Published in the United States by Random House, Inc., New York,
and simultaneously in Canada by Random House of Canada Limited, Toronto.
www.randomhouse.com/seussville www.universalstudios.com
Library of Congress Cataloging-in-Publication Data
Gikow, Louise. Dr. Seuss' how the Grinch stole Christmas! movie storybook /
adapted by Louise Gikow from the motion picture screenplay by Jeffrey Price & Peter S. Seaman.
p. cm.
SUMMARY: Relates the life story of the Grinch, who survives a boisterous childhood
and almost ruins Christmas for the Whos of Whoville.
ISBN 0-375-81103-6
[1. Christmas—Fiction.] I. How the Grinch stole Christmas! (Motion picture : 2000). II. Title.
PZ7.G369 Dt 2000 [Fic]—dc21 00-032340
Printed in the United States of America October 2000 10 9 8 7 6 5 4 3 2 1

It was three days, sixteen hours, and 32 minutes before Christmas, and every Who in Whoville who wasn't trimming a tree or decking a hall was out shopping—including Cindy Lou Who and her father, Lou Lou Who.

Lou loved Christmas shopping. All Whos did. Except for Cindy Lou, who, like many young people, was beginning to question things.

And one of the big things she was questioning was the true meaning of the holiday. *Was Christmas really about buying and giving presents, or was there more to it than that?* Cindy Lou didn't need or want anything from Santa Claus. In fact, the idea of buying someone another snoozlephone just didn't seem very important.

But Cindy Lou's brothers, Drew and Stu, knew exactly what was important. They had decided to play hooky from school and climb Mt. Crumpit with Junie and Christina in search of some mistletoe.

"Where *are* we?" asked Junie as they tramped up the mountain, past the Old Whoville Dump. "I think we should go back."

"What are you—afraid of the *Grinch?"* Stu said with a laugh.

Of course, they all were. Every Who in Whoville was afraid of the Grinch. He had a terrible reputation. And he lived, they say, in a vast, dark cave at the very tippy-top of Mt. Crumpit—exactly where the teens were headed.

"There's no such thing as the Grinch," said Junie.

The furry green figure behind the periscope snickered when he heard this, for he made it his business to know everything that went on on Mt. Crumpit. And he had a whole slew of gizmos and devices to help him spy—and keep Mt. Crumpit blessedly free of Whos.

"Four Whos, one Grinch," he muttered to his faithful dog, Max. "I'll take those odds."

When they arrived at last at the top of the mountain, wheezing and out of breath, the Who teens found a door set into the rock. Beneath the door lay a mat—an "unwelcome" mat, that is.

"It doesn't look like anyone lives here," said Stu, who was in a hurry to get back to Whoville.

But he was wrong. The Grinch lived there. The door creaked open. A hideous monster sprang at them.

The teens raced down the mountain, screaming at the top of their lungs.

They never could say exactly what they saw. Except that whatever it was, it certainly had a *lot* of teeth.

The news was soon all over town—the teens had experienced their first-ever Grinch sighting! (At least that's what they *thought* they saw.) Nobody in Whoville was pleased to hear this. *It was, after all, only three days until the Christmas Eve Whobilation!*

Lou Lou Who just shrugged it off.

"You know how kids are," he told Mayor August May Who. "I'm sure the kids didn't see any Grinch."

The Mayor just shuddered.

But Cindy Lou wasn't frightened. She was curious. "Dad, who's the Grinch?" she asked on the way to school.

"We'll talk about that later," said her father. "You've got to get to class."

Cindy had asked a very good question—even if she didn't get an answer. Just who *was* the Grinch? Some Whos thought he was a Who who'd gone bad. Others thought...well, who knows? Most Whos didn't like to think about him at all.

But every Who in Whoville was certain of this: the Grinch hated Christmas. The whole Christmas season.

And Cindy Lou Who was one Who who was determined to find out the reason why.

Whoville Elementary School was not so very different from the school you go to...except that the most important subject they studied all year-round was—you guessed it—Christmas. They studied from *The Book of Who,* where rules and regulations for Wholiday celebrations were set down in black-and-white and red-and-green. It was time for the students at Whoville Elementary School to announce the themes they'd chosen for their Wholiday reports.

"The Origins of Santy Claus," said one Who girl.

"Gift-Wrapping Oddly Shaped Presents," said another Who.

"Christmas Wreaths: How Many Are *Too* Many?" said a Who boy.

"The Grinch and Why He Doesn't Like Christmas," said Cindy Lou.

At that, every window shade in the room snapped up. Every jaw dropped open.

"Cindy Lou Who!" gasped the teacher, Miss Rue Who. "We do *not* discuss that sort of thing in school!"

That very day, Miss Rue Who called Mr. Lou Lou Who. She demanded he come to his daughter's classroom promptly after school.

"Mr. Lou Who, your daughter," Miss Rue Who sputtered, "she...well, she said...oh my..." Miss Rue Who was so scandalized, words failed to come to her lips.

Lou Lou Who nodded sorrowfully. "I think I know what she said, Miss Rue Who. I'm sure we can straighten this thing out." He turned to his daughter, "Cindy, come help out your old man at the post office, and we'll have a talk."

☆ ☆ ☆

"You see," Lou explained as he stood behind the counter at the post office, helping the first in a long line of Whos get their packages posted in one heck-uva rush, "the Grinch is a Who who...well, he's not really a Who, he's more of a What—that doesn't like Christmas—"

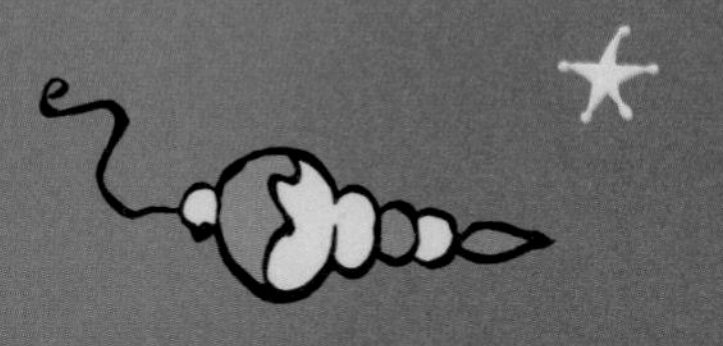

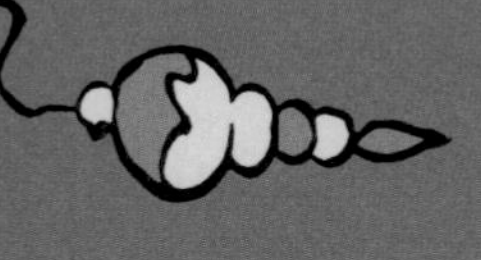

"Oh, Postmaster Lou Who!" cried a voice from the line. It was Mayor May Who.

"Uh-oh," said Lou. He turned to Cindy. "I'm pretty busy right now. Would you mind sorting some mail out back until we can finish our talk?"

Cindy Lou didn't mind. She went in the back and started sorting mail and putting it into slots.

It was a task someone else had already started. But that someone was putting the mail into the wrong slots! And while he was at it, he was sending out fake jury-duty notices, chain letters, and nasty notes.

Who *was* that someone?

That someone was the Grinch!

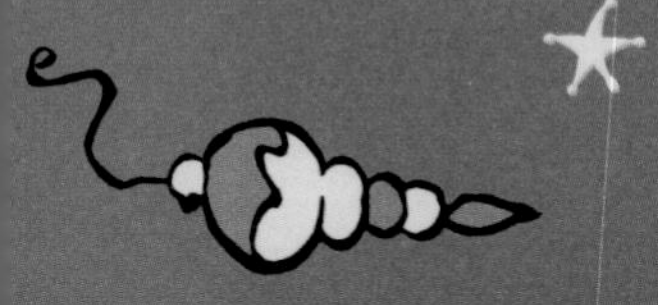

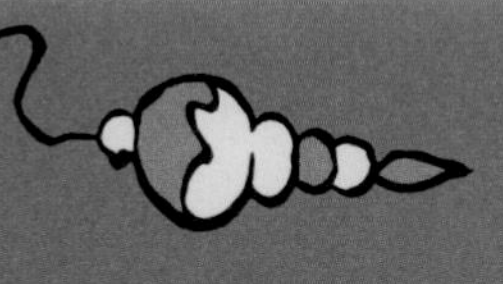

You see, the Grinch didn't always stay up in his cave on Mt. Crumpit. Sometimes he came down to Whoville, cleverly disguised, to make all kinds of Grinchy mischief.

When Cindy Lou caught sight of him, she was so flabbergasted, why, she fell smack into the stamping machine!

She was about to be crushed flat when, against his better judgment, the Grinch surprised himself. He rescued her. He pulled her out of the stamping machine.

Then, before he could leave well enough alone, he wrapped her up like a Christmas present and went on his merry way.

Wasn't Lou surprised when he came in the back in search of his daughter and heard a familiar voice calling to him from a pile of parcels?

After Lou unwrapped his daughter, he and Cindy went home. There, they were not in the least surprised to find Mrs. Betty Lou Who up on the roof, hanging strings of Christmas lights.

You see, each year in Whoville, there was a Christmas lights competition.

And each year, Betty's neighbor Martha May Whovier won the competition. Some Whos said it was because Mayor May Who (who judged the contest) was sweet on Martha May. Some Whos were right!

Nevertheless, Betty was sure that this year she would defeat Martha for the first time ever. The Lou Who house was totally festooned with Christmas lights. It was dazzling, spectacular, a genuine megawatt tour de force. On the outside, at least. The inside was another story. Cindy Lou peered in the front door. "But it's dark inside," she said.

"Feel your way around, dear," called Mrs. Lou Who from up on the roof. "And could you be Mommy's little helper and bring me that light bulb from the refrigerator, too?"

Shaking her head sadly, Cindy entered the darkened house.

The next day, Cindy commenced her report on the Grinch.

She started with an interview with the Who Biddie sisters, Clarinella and Rose. The sisters, Cindy Lou knew, had raised the Grinch from when he was very small.

"How did the Grinch come to you?" Cindy Lou asked. For the interview, she had brought along her tape recorder to record everything that was said.

"He came the way all Who babies come," Clarinella reminisced softly. "On calm nights, they drift down from the sky on little pumbrasellas.

"It was forty years ago this Christmas Eve...We were having our annual Wholiday celebration. It was morning before anybody realized he was out there, the poor dear. We knew right away he was special.

"He was a wonderful little...whatever he was. And we raised him like any other Who child."

Cindy Lou went on to interview Martha May Whovier and Mayor May Who. She found out something that made her very, very sad and a little bit mad. She found out that all the Whos who went to school with the Grinch—especially young May Who—had been very mean to him because he wasn't like them. He was different. Only one Who had been kind. And that Who was Martha. When the Grinch was eight years old, he had been quite sweet on Martha, it seems. He had made a special Christmas present for her. It was an angel that he made of scrap metal and parts he found at the Whoville Dump. He was very proud of it.

So that Christmas Eve, the Grinch went to school with a paper bag on his head, the angel in his hands, and Martha May in his heart.

Miss Rue Who made the Grinch take off the bag. All the children laughed and pointed. You see, the Grinch had tried to shave off his green fur because the other kids had made fun of it. The Grinch's face was covered with nicks and cuts, and he looked, well…even worse than usual.

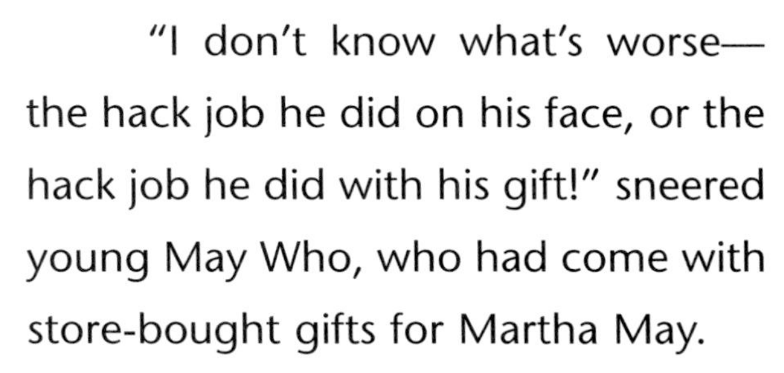

"I don't know what's worse—the hack job he did on his face, or the hack job he did with his gift!" sneered young May Who, who had come with store-bought gifts for Martha May.

In that moment, the Grinch knew he could never fit in with the Whos! He was ugly and green and his present was junky and Martha May would *never* be his. He ran for the door—knocking over the Christmas tree and making a mess of the classroom.

"He never came home that night," Clarinella said, shaking her head sadly.

"In fact," the mayor had also recalled, "that was the last time we ever saw him."

No thanks to you, thought Cindy Lou.

And that's when she hatched her plan.

E·PLURIBUS·WHONUM
WHOBILATION 1000

The next day was Christmas Eve—the day of the annual Christmas Whobilation. Every year, the Whos elected someone to be the Holiday Cheermeister. Cindy Lou nominated the Grinch.

At first, every Who in Whoville was horrified. (Mostly the mayor, because *he* wanted the job.) But Cindy stood her ground. "After all," she said, reading to them from *The Book of Who,* "'The Cheermeister is one who deserves a backslap or a toast. It goes to the soul at Christmas who needs it most!' And I believe that soul is the Grinch."

Cindy Lou looked up at the assembled crowd. "And if you're the Whos I hope you are, you will, too." At first all that could be heard was sniffles. Then the crowd burst into applause.

It was settled. The Grinch would be that year's Cheermeister.

But who was going to tell him?

Cindy climbed Mt. Crumpit and asked the Grinch to be Cheermeister.

And the Grinch, with a little bit of coaxing from his faithful dog, Max, accepted the honor.

With a little more help from Max, the Grinch dressed in his holiday best for the event.

He tried to be a good sport. Really. He did.

He put on the sweater the Who Biddie sisters knitted him, which was five sizes too small. He sat in the Chair of Cheer. He judged the Pudding Cook Off. He led the Christmas Conga Line. He did Vigorous Exercise. He Blessed the Children. He led yet another Christmas Conga Line. He drank gallons of Christmas Nog. And then it came time for the Present Pass It On.

But unfortunately, no one had told the Grinch he needed to bring a present. And that, the Whos learned, was a very big mistake.

Of course, the mayor used the occasion to give Martha May a diamond ring. And a new car.

The Grinch could not help but remember that day back in Whoville Elementary School—the day of his great humiliation. And in a way, he was really reliving that day all over again today. Well, as you can imagine, it was more than the Grinch could bear.

"*That's* what it's always been about, isn't it?" he raved. "*Gifts! Gifts! Gifts!* Well, let me tell you what happens to your gifts: they all end up coming to me—in your garbage—to the dump!"

The hushed Whos watched as the Grinch spun around and headed for Mt. Crumpit. But before he did, a fearful, frightful, fiendish idea stole into his furry green head. Slowly, he turned around. "Oh, I'm a terrible Cheermeister! I forgot to light the tree!" And with that, he lit the tree all right. He set the great Christmas tree in Whoville Square on fire!

Later, back on Mt. Crumpit...

"I've got to do something," the Grinch muttered as he paced the floor of his cave. "I must *stop* this Christmas from coming. *But how?"*

And that's when he came up with an ingenious plan. The crowning achievement of his glorious career as a Christmas kibosher.

First, he needed a reindeer. He looked around. No reindeer. Then he caught sight of Max. Max shrank away. "With some antlers...you'll do fine," the Grinch said with a grin.

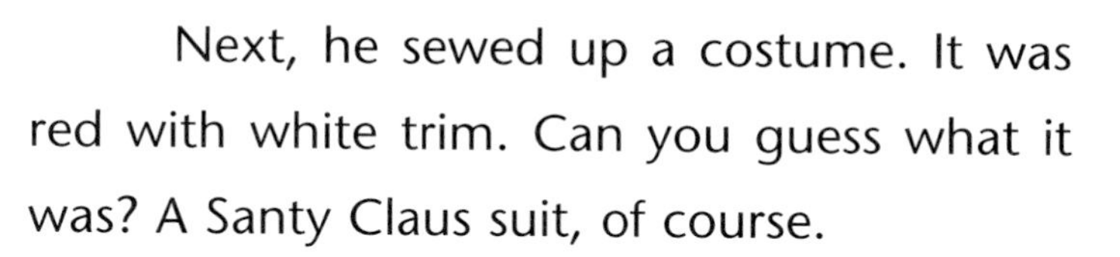

Next, he sewed up a costume. It was red with white trim. Can you guess what it was? A Santy Claus suit, of course.

Then he hitched up Max to a sleigh.

And he was off!

While the Whos down in Whoville were fast asleep in their beds, the fake Santy Claus stole down their chimneys into their houses and took all their presents and all their decorations and stuffed them up their Who chimneys and piled them into his sleigh.

He cleaned out every Who refrigerator and every Who Christmas tree. He even stole their stockings.

It was at the very last house, at Cindy Lou Who's house, while he was stuffing the tree up the chimney, that he almost got caught.

Cindy Lou herself came downstairs at that very moment. She stood there, rubbing her sleepy little eyes. "Santa, what are you doing with our tree?" she asked.

"Uh...there's a light on this tree that won't light on one side," the Grinch lied. "I'm taking it home to my workshop to fix it."

"Santa?" Cindy yawned. "Don't forget the Grinch. I know he's mean and hairy and smelly. But I think he's actually kinda...sweet."

Hearing this, the Grinch gulped.

When the Whos awoke that Christmas morning, they were in for a shock. Everything—their presents, their trees, their decorations, their holiday food—was gone.

In their jammies and slippers, they came together in the town square.

"It was the Grinch!" cried Mayor May Who. "Cindy Lou Who, I hope you're proud of what you've done!"

Cindy Lou shrank from the Mayor's gaze, and a tear fell down her cheek.

But Lou Lou Who stepped up and put his arm around his daughter. "Well, if she isn't proud...*then I am,*" he said. "I'm glad the Grinch took our presents! Because presents are not what Christmas is all about. Gifts and contests and colored lights...I guess that's what Cindy's been trying to tell everyone. *Christmas is about being together with our families and loved ones.* And that's all."

From atop Mt. Crumpit, the Grinch peered down at the Whos. He expected to hear a wail of woe. But instead what did he hear? He heard...the sound of Whos singing a sweet Christmas carol!

The Grinch hadn't stopped Christmas from coming. It had come anyway!

And that very minute, Cindy Lou Who was coming up Mt. Crumpit to ask the Grinch to join the Whos' celebration.

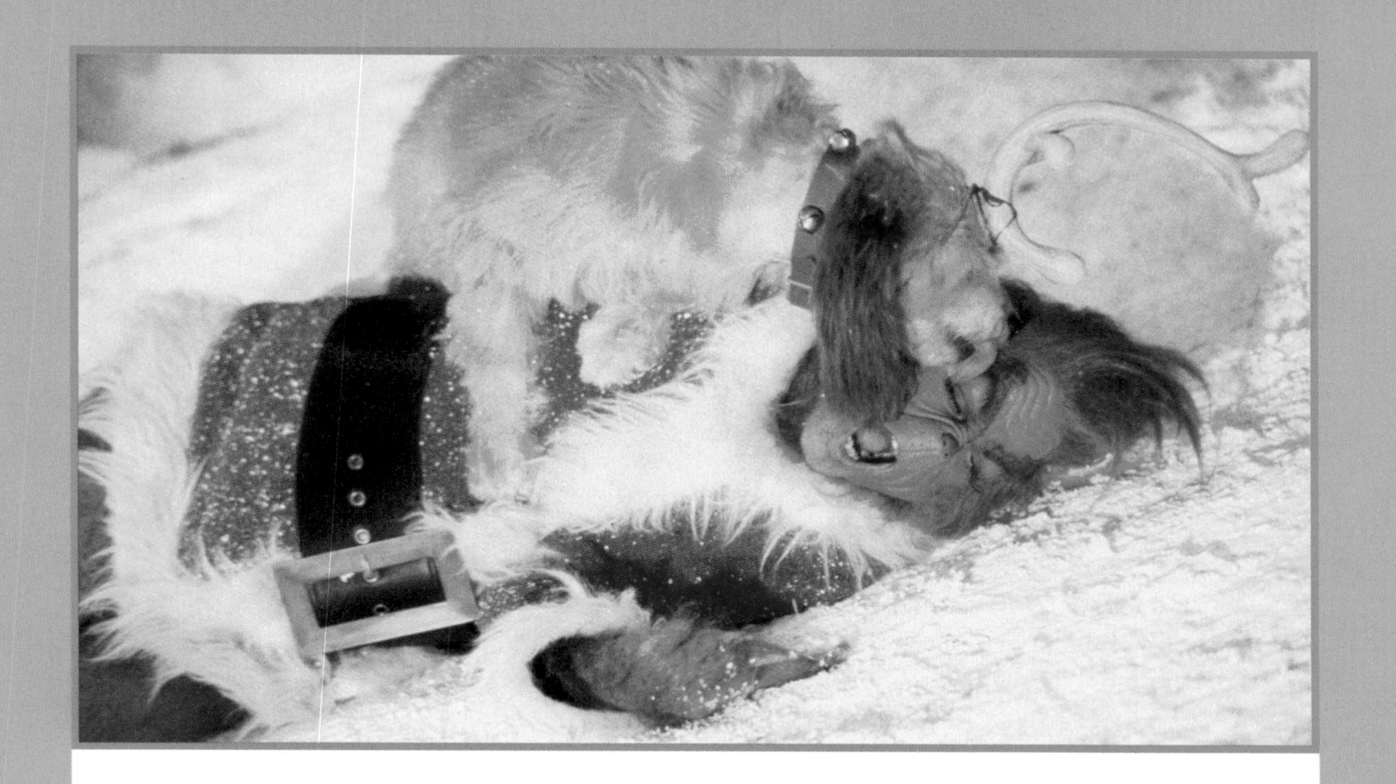

In spite of himself, the Grinch felt something warm swell in his chest. What was it? Can you guess? No one is quite sure, but the Whos think it might have been his heart: his cold, hard little Grinchy heart just might have started to grow.

The Grinch, Max, and Cindy Lou flew down the hillside in the Grinch's sleigh, the Whos' Christmas presents and decorations and stockings and food jouncing in the great big bag behind them.

They came to a screeching halt in the middle of Whoville Square.

"Well, what have we here?" asked Officer Wholihan.

"Ya got me, Officer. I did it," the Grinch confessed. "I am the Grinch who stole Christmas. And I am sorry."

But the Whos were in no mood to punish the Grinch (excepting the mayor, to whom no Who listened, anyhow!).

And that Christmas Day ended up being the happiest that the Whos—and the Grinch—had ever known.

Merry Grinch-mas to all!